Virtual Maniac
Silly and Serious Poems for Kids

by Margriet Ruurs

Illustrated by Eve Tanselle

To Ben
Have fun reading!

Margriet R

Cover Art and Illustrations: Eve Tanselle
Book Design: Maria Messenger

Canadian children's author Margriet Ruurs is available for school visits and speaking appearances throughout North America. Reach her at ruur@junction.net, or through the publisher.

Eve Tanselle is a Florida artist. She can be reached through Maupin House Publishing.

Maupin House Publishing, Inc. publishes classroom-proven professional resources for K-12 language arts teachers.

Contact us at 1-800-524-0634, 352-373-5588, or at www.maupinhouse.com to learn more about our resources or quality, on-site staff development.

Library of Congress Cataloging-in-Publication Data

Ruurs, Margriet.
    Virtual maniac / Margriet Ruurs ; illustrated by Eve Tanselle.
        p. cm.
    ISBN 978-0-929895-43-7   ISBN 0-929895-43-6
    1. Children's poetry, Canadian. [1. Canadian poetry.] I. Tanselle, Eve, ill. II. Title.

PR9199.3.R86 V57 2000
811'.54--dc21
                                                                    00-060579

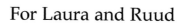

For Laura and Ruud

Contents

Words in My Head

Words are walking through my head
as I lie in bed
waiting for sleep,
the words leap,
march, stumble,
play hide and seek.

Sometimes the words walk
in sentences,
making stories as they stalk
through my head.

I try to close the tap
but the words just flow,
in line they step
and just won't go.

I wait for dreams.
Then, when I wake,
the stories scatter here and there
and I can't find them anywhere.

I try to make
the words walk back and forth,
leaving footprints in my brain
so I will find them back again.

Virtual Maniac

A strange thing happened to me!
I'm not sure how, but you see
my mom rented me a video game...
Since then I haven't been the same.

We rented it just for one day.
I thought it was awesome, yelled, "Hurray!"
I chose cool games that looked all right,
with race cars, swords and a black knight.

I carried the machine home and into my room...
It instantly changed into a temple of doom!
I switched on machine and TV
and a strange thing happened to me.

I changed! From a nice kid into a blob!
My thumbs could only push each little knob,
my eyes were fixed onto the screen,
I looked like the fenziest frantic that you've ever seen!

Just sat there punching, transfixed,
moving little men, boxes and sticks.
I didn't eat or drink or go to the loo...
It was weird. Did it ever happen to you?

Sometimes I yelled, "No!" or screamed, "Hey!"
My mom came running to see if I was okay.
My ears heard only bleep-bleep-bleep.
I didn't even take time out to sleep!

The controls seemed glued to my hands
as I pushed the video game's commands.
I forgot what time it was, what day.
All I did was sit and push "play."

Then all of a sudden, I came back to life.
It happened the next day, just before five.
My mom pulled the plug! I couldn't play anymore,
The machine had to go back to the store!

Green

Frogs 'n
pea soup,
a stormy sea,
weeds 'n
broccoli!

Lily pads,
forests
bushy bamboo
lettuce leaves
and envy, too!

Yellow

Sunshine is yellow
and so is chicken soup.
Bright yellow are my markers,
the chicks in the chicken coop.

My dancing mood is yellow,
I have a yellow dress.
Butterflies and daffodils,
dandelions in the grass!

Yellow is the springtime,
golden honey on my toast.
And in a waving field of flowers
I like yellow ones the most!

Owls in the Woods

I was walking through the woods
on a quiet spring day.
New leaves filtered sunlight
waving my worries away.

Then suddenly...I startled
at an owl's hollow hoot!
The sunny silence shattered
as twigs crushed underfoot.

There...just steps ahead,
two owlets huddled by a tree,
hiding in their furry feathers,
huge eyes stared at me.

Their mother warned, from up above,
they knew that she was near
and never blinked or quivered
or otherwise showed fear.

I quietly retreated
and smiled up at the sky.
We shared a springtime secret,
those little owls and I.

7

Unique

Sometimes
I see myself
through different eyes.
Sometimes
I realize
that how I see
and how I speak
is me.
Unique.

Gotta Go!

I gotta go, I gotta go so bad
I think I'm gonna float!
If I don't find a bathroom soon
I think I will explode.

If I have yet another drink
and my bladder still expands
or hear one more drop of water in the sink
I **know** I'll pee in my pants!

Argillaceous

I don't quite know
if it's something that hurts
or a place to go.
All I know
is that I **like** words
like argillaceous.
Words like that are delicious!
I can say it, see it, smell it
and I can even learn to spell it!

Argillaceous means soil containing clay.
Pronounce: arg-ill-AA-cee-us

10

Downhill

Like a bird in the sky
I soar down the slope
faster and faster, I hope
I get wings and can fly!

Scratching white snow,
trees flying by,
faster and faster I go;
an eagle in the sky.

Soaring on wings
down the white slope,
wind in my ears sings
of flying, of dreams and of hope.

Cat Love

I rub against your leg,
stumble all over your toes.
Itching, twitching tail,
rub my rubber nose.

I love you so,
I purr, prefer you.
Now I'll move on and show
how much I love the table leg!

Crushed

I really, truly think that
gorgeous Chrissy from 7B,
whose looks drive me mad,
has a serious crush on me!

The way she looks,
the way she walks,
the way she holds her books
and giggles when she talks...

I know for sure she's got a crush!
Just saw her at the dance.
'Twas pretty dark but I saw her blush.
and decide to take my chance.

Casually, I saunter over there,
give her my most attractive grin.
She swings around, twirling blonde hair,
and lands a mighty upper on my chin!

The Truth About Bruce

Have you seen my dog Bruce?
Let me tell you, it's the truth...
That dog is very, very strong,
it's true, don't get me wrong.
My dog can lift up City Hall,
city council, mayor and all!!

Have you seen my dog Bruce?
Well, let me tell you the truth...
That dog is **so** very smart
he knows the alphabet by heart,
and not just our ABCs
but also in Chinese!

Have you seen my dog Bruce?
Would I tell you anything but the truth?
That dog is so cool
he can drink a whole pool!
Eats hamburgers every day
from a silver serving tray.

Have you never seen Bruce, my dog?
He honestly uses a log
for a toothpick, it's no tale
and when he wags his tail
it storms all over the city!
You haven't seen him? What a pity....
My dog Bruce knows every trick.

He can sit and fetch a stick,
roll over and play dead —
he is very good at **that!**
Once he played dead for seven
days!
I say, "Stay!" and Bruce stays!

When Bruce barks, plug your ears —
you can hear him in Algiers!
Windows shatter, towers shake,
people everywhere awake
When Bruce barks, burglars flee —
Now, why would you not believe me!?

You **haven't** seen Bruce?
Well, let me tell you the truth...
    I'm not surprised at that...
        you see, I just saw a cat.
        I'm pretty sure Bruce went to hide...

        ...because of cats he's terrified!

Kleena Kleene

Kleena Kleene, Takla, Tatlayoko,
Bella Coola, Bella Bella
Archennini, Wapa Wekka, Flin Flon.
This is not a song!
So listen 'n listen well:
Mingo, Orem, Lusk 'n Twisp.
No, it's not a spell!
Babble, Boon, Dasher, Dunlap,
All are places on the map!

Polkas and Perogies

My father is Irish, my mother is Greek,
you can tell by their accent when they start to speak.
Granny's from England, Uncle from Uruguay
and we all live in the U. S. of A.!

We sing songs from all over the world,
different languages can often be heard
when we have a party with family and friends,
they're all people who came from different lands.

We eat perogies and eggrolls with cheese,
dance polkas and sing in Chinese.
We are a mish-mash, hodgepodge family —
and that's the best way to be!

Anna-Belle-Lou

A girl named Anna-Belle-Lou
said: "I don't like my hair blonde, I want it blue!"
She painted her hair, not orange or green
but the bluest blue that you've ever seen!

She went for a walk and the birds squeaked, "Hi..."
are you a piece of clear blue sky?"
She looked heavenly, it's true,
her hair was so unbelievably blue!

She walked by a pond and a voice said:
"Is that water on top of your head?"
A bellowing beaver and a giggling otter
mistook her hair for crystal blue water!

A little while later she met a bear,
a hungry bear who looked at her hair.
"Blueberries!" he hollered with glee,
but Anna-Belle-Lou said: "No, dumbo, it's me!"

She went home feeling sadder than sad
with a hanging, very blue head.
Her mother saw the curls of Anna-Belle-Lou
and said, "I like it! I **like** your hair blue!"

That did it! It was more than she could take,
maybe her blue hair was just a mistake,
thought Anna-Belle-Lou, who now can be seen
with a hairdo fluorescent bright green!

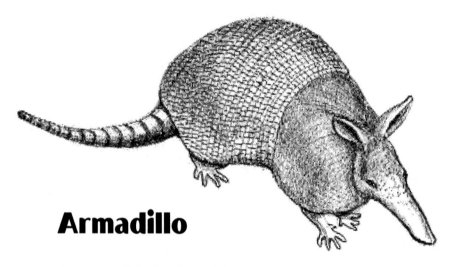

Armadillo

An armadillo in Amarillo
said, "No,
I don't want to be in a fashion show!
I'm not interested
in being a beauty contestant.
I guess I might have been keener
if I looked less like a vacuum cleaner."

By the Light of the Moon

Do you know what elk do
by the light of the moon?
They boogie-woogie together
and bugle a tune!

Do you know what bears do
at night by the moon's fading light?
Make lots of snowballs to have
a big bear snowball fight!

Do you know what moose do
when the night is still?
They sit on their antlers
and toboggan downhill!

Old Growth Kleenex

For six hundred years he stood
in the valley he guarded,
to be turned into tissues
that will be discarded.

Dragons in the Sky

There are dragons in the sky
fleetingly floating by.
Their bulging bellies billow
lumpy, bumpy as my pillow.

As they flap gigantic wings
each sailing, scaly dragon swings.
They blink, they wink as if it's a joke
and then they slowly slink to smoke.

School Sick

I **don't** want to go to school today.
I think I'll be sick so I can stay
in my bed, cozy and warm.
I **don't** want to go out in rain and storm.
I'll throw up all over the rug
and crawl back to bed, comfy 'n snug.

I'll fake a sore throat and a fever.
My mom is smart, but I can deceive her!
I'll have funny lumps with a rash
so she'll want me back in bed in a flash.
That way I can stay home and play,
slumber and snooze the entire day.

Uh oh!
Here comes my mom with a bottle and a pill,
she takes my temperature, I have to lie very still!
I don't want to swallow **that!**
I just may have to get out of bed!
The medicine has a terrible smell,
and all of a sudden I feel very well!

Big Bullies

There are bullies in our school
and they think they are so cool.
Super Simon, Krazy Kevin
and Big Billy in Grade Seven
want to pick a fight with me
every day, after three.

I think they have a kind of club
and they want to beat me up.
I don't know exactly why,
maybe 'cause I'm kind of shy...

I've decided they are sad
so I simply shake my head.
I don't know what to say
but it's hard to just walk away.

Some days my hands are itching
and I'm tempted to go snitching.
But then I'd be just like them: a fool.
So, those bullies in my school
I don't even try to beat or barter:
I just **know** that I am smarter!

Rainbow Rock

I found a rock, a rock of many colors
with purple, blue and green.
A special rock, the best rock I've ever seen.

My rock, this rock of many colors, I hold
and tilt it in the light.
Some spots are emerald blue
and specks of silver, too.
There's tulip red and marigold
and gold flakes sparkling bright.

My rock, this precious rock, it has a special glow.
I am pretty sure that what it is
is one small piece of rainbow.

Campfire Time

The crackling campfire dances
with long, licking flames,
while we sing silly songs
and play a million games.

Snapping, crackling twigs
compete with blazing fire
as dancing firefly sparks
fly higher and higher.

Teasing, threatening,
golden tongues lick
at the dark of night
and at my marshmallow stick.

If I Were the Teacher

If I were the teacher, I'd say, "Okay, class,
that's it, no more math!"
I'd put an end to the spelling test
and always be right 'cause the teacher knows best!
If I were the teacher, we'd have recess
from eight-thirty till eleven, I guess
Maybe till eleven-thirty!
It's okay if our shoes are dirty.
We wouldn't have to hang up our coat and hat
or to say, "Excuse me," and all that.
No more science or social studies!
Me and my students would really be buddies.
Just comics to read, cartoons to see!
Each desk would have its own color TV!
No homework, never, ever.
We'd automatically get clever,
just look at a book and we'd know
subtraction and fractions and so!

If I were the teacher, I'd order pizza for lunch!
Popcorn and cookies for the students to munch!
We would write on the walls
and run down the halls...
But...I might get in trouble for, after all,
even a teacher has to listen to the principal!

A Piece of History

I went for a walk on a hill,
the forest was quiet and still.
Listened to wind in the trees,
the murmur of water, humming of bees.

Sometimes I need to be all alone...
Tossed a rock, picked up a stone,
turned it over, all smooth and round
it was then that a treasure I found.

A fossil...tiny and gray.
Once it had lived, then faded away.
Now I could see its shape and its bone,
preserved forever in this tiny stone.

Eons faded as I looked at this gift,
testimony to what had once lived.
The forest grew quiet and still
as I touched history, there on that hill.

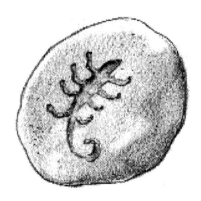

Singing

I **like** making music with my voice
with notes in high and low.
It's such a joyful, cheerful noise

I wonder why my brother hates it so!

Marcus P. Pringle

Marcus P. Pringle was just one of the boys,
liked soccer and pizza and all kinds of toys.
Marcus P. Pringle was an ordinary guy,
not a big bully but really quite shy.
He had freckles, hair that was spiked,
and a friendly grin that everyone liked.
Marcus P. Pringle did just fine in school,
liked to go for a dive in the pool.
In short, Marcus P. Pringle, you see
was a normal kid, just like you and me.

But...

Marcus P. Pringle did have one fault.
It started in a cardshop, so I am told.
A friend took him there, his best friend Jim
talked Marcus into coming with him.
Marcus looked around the store,
saw hockey cards piled from ceiling to floor...
cards in boxes, cards everywhere.
Marcus P. Pringle just stood staring there.

While he stood staring at each little card
he felt a strange tingle down in his heart.
After that he was totally lost, I swear it,
Marcus P. Pringle became a hockey card addict!
Bought cards, bargained and traded,
only quality cards, nothing crumpled or faded.
Had rookie cards from everyone, ever
At trading he became very clever.

Soon he had more cards than anyone in his class,
kept what he needed and traded the rest.
Stored cards, first in his desk in a box,
then in his locker with his sneakers and socks.

When his locker was full
he had more cards than anyone in the school.
Soon Marcus stored cards under his bed.
It didn't take long before his mother said,
"Marcus, please move to the shed!"
Marcus moved, taking his cards and his bed.

Day and night he traded without slowing down,
soon he had more cards than anyone in town.
He traded his lunch for Mark Messier's rookie,
traded a Howe for a chocolate chip cookie.
He wanted a Gretzky upperdeck, wanted it bad
so he traded his sister for that!
By the time he had

LeMieux, Hull and Murray
Marcus P. Pringle started to worry.
What if his cards got stolen or lost?
How much were they worth, how much did they cost?
What if a tornado came through the shed
and carried away his cards from under his bed?
What if the Flames went up in flames, oh no!
What if the team let Messier go?

He worried so much his spiked hair went flat,
his teachers and parents and friends shook their heads.
Then one little girl, she was in grade three,
stepped up to Marcus and said, "Now listen to me,
your collecting has definitely gone to your head,
we've had enough, this is it, that is that!
No more cards, not one, not even a trophy.
It got out of hand, don't you see?"

Marcus P. Pringle sat down in perplextion.
"And what," did he ask, "should I do with my collection?"
"That's easy," said the girl from grade three,
"Just give them away and you'll see
that you won't worry about cards anymore,
just share them, that's what collections are for!"
So Marcus handed out cards, ten thousand a day,
he actually enjoyed giving them away.
He gave to his family and to each friend,
gave away his collection without any end.

Gave away from his locker and box
and after a week he saw his socks!
Moved back in the house with his bed
no longer needed to live in the shed.
He felt so much better, Marcus P. Pringle,
as he was giving away every single
card he had ever collected
and said, "It feels better than I ever expected!"

"No more collecting for me, never, ever!"
Marcus P. Pringle learned the hard way and got clever.
He vowed never again a collection to start
never to touch another hockey card!
And he didn't.

But...

Two weeks later Marcus P. Pringle
felt in his heart a strange little tingle
His head spinned, his hands went damp
as he stared at a rare, foreign stamp...

Fall Feelings

Have you **felt** the Fall?
Its frosty tongue
licking your fingers and toes,
Its cold breath
nipping at your nose.

Have you **heard** the Fall?
Geese honking good-bye,
flying south again.
Leaves trickling off the trees
like red and yellow rain.

Have you **seen** the Fall?
Its golden torches
lighting up everything,
its blanket of brown,
tucking in the world until next spring.

Freedom of Thought

If ever I am chained in a tower
and never be set free
I'd still have all the power
to choose my destiny.

If ever I'm confined to bed,
or destined to a chair
I'll ride the horse in my head
and gallop...anywhere!

Remembering

I remember when we went to play
on a snowy hill and took the sleigh.
I swooshed right down...
I remember a town,
the lights, the sights, the sounds, the smells.
I remember it all, remember it well.

I remember a horse, of course,
I remember a cow and the cat's meow.

It was on a farm
I remember the arm
that gave me a hug
when our truck got stuck.

I remember a sweet, smiling face,
we went to that funny place,
there was a slide and a swing...
Oh! I remember everything!

Now, what did I have to get in this store?
I just can't remember anymore.

Winter Weather

Minus ten was getting nippy,
Minus twenty my nose was drippy!
Minus thirty, I needed mitts.
Minus forty was the pits!
Minus fifty and I froze,
icicles hanging from my nose!
Minus sixty, what a scare —
time to put on long underwear!

Phone Poem

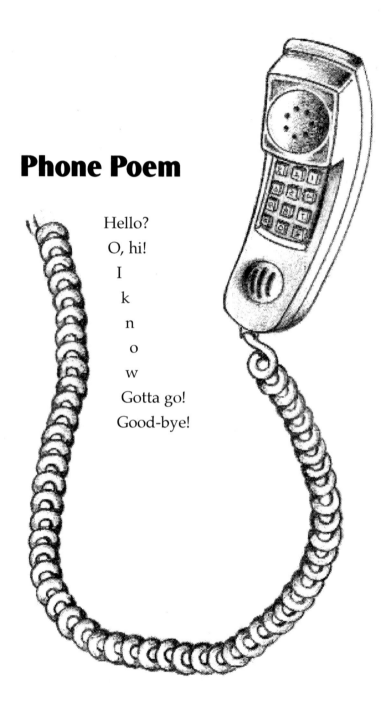

Hello?
O, hi!
I
  k
    n
      o
        w
Gotta go!
Good-bye!

Puppy Love

Hello, world, here I am,
I came to chew your laces,
to lick your nose in puppy love
and have you tumble races!

Are you ready for me, world?
I'll make puddles on your floor.
I'll chew your shoes to pieces
and whimper at your door.

Sometimes I'll need a cuddle,
this world seems awfully big —
and I am still so very small.
Give me a hug, and I'll give you a lick!

Brother

My brother is so mean...
the meanest, miserablest brat you've ever seen!
He filled the toothpaste tube with glue
and tied my laces — shoe to shoe!
He feeds his supper to the dog
and in his lunch kit lives a frog.

My brother is so mean...
He really is a mean machine!
He broke a favorite toy of mine,
he likes to cry and wail and whine.
Keeps spiders as his pets,
barks at dogs and chases cats.

My brother is **so** mean...
the strangest boy you've ever seen!
He flushed my marbles down the drain,
runs down the hallway like a train.
I think he teaches Frankenstein...
that bratty brother of mine!

Stagefright

Faces, like pale moons
setting
beyond the blinding light

Restless feet, like leaves
shuffling,
a cough, a sigh.

Expectant eyes, like stars
winking
in a sky of black.

A deep breath, voice and hands
trembling,
then slowly, it all comes back.

Traveling

When I grow old and gray
I'd like to travel every day
to see the earth from every side,
I'd like to travel far and wide.

But that is still some time from now,
I wonder if somehow
the earth then will still be
as beautiful to see.
Pollution layers, acid rain,

peace missions all in vain...
Will people learn to save the earth
and will they try for all it's worth?

Will oak trees grow and rivers flow?
Will deer and elk still roam,
will earth still be our only home?

When I am old and gray
I'd like to see the world someday.
To see the earth from every side
I'd like to travel far and wide.

Moose Meadow

In May in Manitoba
in the middle of a meadow
is a muddy marsh.

In the middle of that muddy meadow marsh
in the month of May in Manitoba,
a mighty moose munches
on a meal of maple leaves!

Knight Time

If I were a knight I'd have a white horse
and wear a suit of armor, of course.
I'd rescue a maiden with golden hair.
There'd be nothing that I wouldn't dare.

I'd ride through the land,
ask a princess for her hand.
The king would give me his throne
and I'd conquer dragons all alone!

If I were a knight in medieval days
I'd behave in medieval ways.
Things would be fun, I suppose,
but I'd need a can opener to get out of my clothes!

Yuck!

I'm not particularly picky
but I **hate** gum that is sticky.
I'll blow a bubble, pop it goes,
sticky pink all over my nose!

I **hate** chewy green beans
and we always have them, it seems.
I **hate** broccoli that goes crunch
and I **hate** cucumbers in my lunch!

I **hate** sisters who kiss,
I **hate** snakes that hiss,
I **hate** a shower when it's cold,
I **hate** doing as I'm told!

I **hate** mosquitoes in the house
and my green and purple blouse.
I **hate** slimy, yucky slugs
and creepy crawly little bugs!

Sometimes I hate everything!
Don't want to do anything.
Then I just kind of stomp away
on such a hating-things-kind-of-day.

Smelly Poem

My favorite kind of perfume
is a barnyard kitten, a lilac in bloom.
The smell of freshly cut hay
on a warm summer day,
the dusty sweet scent
of rain as it falls on the land.
Comforting smells of a horse in the stable,
welcoming wafts from food on the table.
The aroma of a sky full of rainbows
and velvety flowers that tickle my nose!

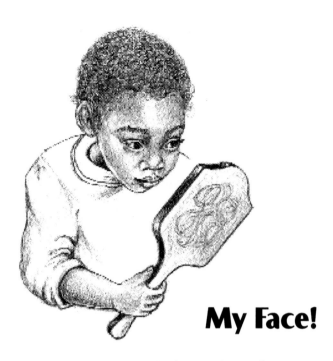

My Face!

It's funny, but when you're small
people don't think it's you at all!
They take one look and say, "Oh, gee,
she looks just like her aunt Marie."
They say I have my grandpa's nose,
but it sure sounds different when **he** blows!

My face, they say, I have from Mom,
my eyes are from my brother Tom.
My hair I have from my sister Shirley
but I don't **want** mine to be so curly!

When I look in the mirror I see...
well...I just see ME!

Mouse Mousse

My cat Mimi likes gourmet,
savors smoked salmon paté,
mouse mousse and fish filet,
lobster bake and shrimp saté.

My cat Mimi loves to munch
caviar crackers for her lunch.
She has been invited, wow!
for a special feline chow
with the First Cat at the White House.
We are working on her manners now.

Meouwww!

Mimi!

Don't talk with mouse mousse in your mouth!

Wishful Spider

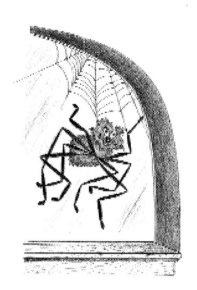

There once was a spider on the wall
who'd spun a web but didn't like it at all.
She knew how to catch beetles and flies
but sighed, "I'd much rather have burgers and fries!"

She lived outside on a beautiful home
by a window shaped like a dome.
Peeking inside at fine furniture and rugs,
she sighed, "That beats windy webs and bugs!"

One night, when the people sat on the deck
the spider slid down close to a neck.
She hung there, on a silvery thread,
wishfully looking at all that they had.

While the lady sat sipping her cider,
she lowered herself, our brave little spider.
She wanted to see the pearl necklace up close
and felt the touch of those satiny clothes.

She wanted so badly to be more than a spider,
to fulfill all the dreams living inside her.
More than a bug with eight legs and no ears.
But the lady had other ideas, it appears!

The thread was long, right down to the back,
when the spider stepped off, onto the neck,
admiring the pearls, just like in a dream
until she heard a bloodcurdling scream!

There was a swoop of a hand in the neck
and the spider fell down on the deck.
A fine leather shoe followed, the stomp of a foot
but eight tiny legs made the spider scoot.

Never again did she go near,
pearls and satin are now something to fear...
People live in homes, sipping cider,
but webs and bugs are just fine for a spider!

Cookies

When I need a snack
I like to take a bulging bag
of cookies, my far most favorite flavor:
chocolate-chip-vanilla-cream!
I have this re-occurring dream
that all I get for lunch
is cookies to munch.

Bags 'n stacks 'n racks of my favorites:
ginger-maple-raisin-fudge flavorites!
At tea time I don't need tea,
cookies is all you have to give me.
If you really wanna do me a favor
give me my most-delicious, frumentaceous flavor:
peanut-butter-oatmeal-sugar-and-spice!
It may not make me any thinner,
but what I want for breakfast, lunch and dinner
is crispy
crunchy
crumbly
cookies!

The Ocean

A giant dragon
breathing foam
on rocky, green toes.

It roars,
then softly rumbles,
retreats to attack again.

It gathers misty breath
and strength
to roar back with all its might
and eat away at sand and caves,
its belly softly rumbling.

It rests.
Gray back panting, heaving,
rise and fall, it slumbers
then wakes again and roars,
spitting foam and salty mist.

Treasure Chest

Open the cover of the book in your hands,
bridge to unknown and wonderful lands.
Travel through countries of wisdom and fun,
nights full of darkness, days full of sun.

Turn each page full of wonder,
follow its road to up yonder
where mountain tops talk to the sky
whispering a wondering "why?"

Treasure chest of make-believe places,
meeting new and familiar faces.
Reach for a book on the shelf —
Discover the world, discover yourself.